Japanese Children's Favorite Stories

Book Two

Japanese Children's Favorite Stories

Book Two

Compiled by Florence Sakade
Illustrated by Yoshio Hayashi

TUTTLE PUBLISHING
Boston • Rutland, Vermont • Tokyo

Published by Tuttle Publishing,
an imprint of Periplus Editions (HK) Ltd with editorial offices at
153 Milk Street, Boston, Massachusetts 02109
and 130 Joo Seng Road, #06-01, Singapore 368357

First printing, 2004
© 2004 by Periplus Editions (HK) Ltd.

LCC Card No. 2003109579
ISBN 0-8048-3381-8

Printed in Singapore

Distributed by:

Japan
Tuttle Publishing
Yaekari Building, 3F
5-4-12 Osaki, Shinagawa-ku,
Tokyo 141-0032
Tel: (03) 5437 0171 Fax: (03) 5437 0755
Email: tuttle-sales@gol.com

North America, Latin America & Europe
Tuttle Publishing
Airport Industrial Park
364 Innovation Drive
North Clarendon, VT 05759-9436
Tel: (802) 773 8930 Fax: (802) 773 6993
Email: info@tuttlepublishing.com

Asia Pacific
Berkeley Books Pte Ltd
130 Joo Seng Road #06-01
Singapore 368357
Tel: (65) 6280 1330 Fax: (65) 6280 6290
Email: inquiries@periplus.com.sg

09 08 07 06 05 04
6 5 4 3 2 1

Contents

The Magic Mortar

Once upon a time two brothers lived together in a little village in Japan. The eldest brother worked very hard all the time, but the younger brother was very lazy and good-for-nothing. One day the elder brother went off to the mountains to work. While he was working, an old man came up to him and gave him a mortar made of stone, the kind used for grinding rice or wheat into flour.

"This is a magic mortar which will give you anything you wish for," said the old man. "Please take it home with you."

The elder brother was very happy and rushed home with the mortar.

"Please give me rice. We need rice." So saying, he ground the stick in the mortar. And all at once out came rice, bales of rice. There was so much that he gave rice to everyone in the village.

"This is wonderful! This is a great help. Thank you very much." The villagers were all very happy.

That is, everyone was happy except the lazy younger brother. "I wish I had that; I'd make better use of it," he grumbled to himself. And one day he stole the magic mortar and ran away.

"No one will be able to catch me if I can get to the ocean," he thought as he ran to the seashore.

When he reached the shore, he found a small rowboat. He took it and rowed very hard out to sea. He soon was far out and right in the middle of the big waves.

Then he stopped rowing and began to think what he wanted to ask the mortar for. "I have it! I would like a lot of nice, sweet little cakes." And he began to grind at the mortar with the stick. "Give me cake! Give me cake!" And lots of fine white cakes came rolling out of the mortar.

"My! How good they are! And what a lot of cakes I got!" And he ate everyone. He had eaten so many and they were so sweet that he began to feel like he wanted to eat something salty to take the too-sweet taste out of his mouth.

So he ground at the mortar again and said: "Give me salt this time. I want salt. I want salt." And now salt came pouring out of the mortar, all white and shining. And it kept coming and coming.

"Enough," he cried, "I've had enough. Stop!" But the salt kept coming and coming, and the boat began to fill up and get heavy. And still the salt kept coming, and now the boat was so full it started to sink. And as the brother sank with the boat, he was still crying: "Enough! Enough!"

But the mortar kept on giving out salt and more salt, even down at the bottom of the ocean, and it is still doing it. And that is why the sea is salty.

How to Fool a Cat

Once upon a time there was a rich lord who liked to collect carvings of animals. He had many kinds, but he had no carved mouse. So he called two skilled carvers to him and said:

"I want each of you to carve a mouse for me. I want them to be so lifelike that my cat will think they're real mice and pounce on them. We'll put them down together and see which mouse the cat pounces on first. To the carver of that mouse I'll give this bag of gold."

So the two carvers went back to their homes and set to work. After a time they came back. One had carved a wonderful mouse out of wood. It was so well done that it looked exactly like a mouse. The other, however, had done very badly. He had used some material that flaked and looked funny; it didn't look like a mouse at all.

"What's this?" asked the lord. "This wooden mouse is a marvelous piece of carving, but this other mouse—if it is indeed supposed to be a mouse—wouldn't fool anyone, let alone a cat."

"Let the cat be brought in," said the second carver. "The cat can decide which is the better mouse."

The lord thought this was rather silly, but he ordered the cat to be brought in. No sooner had it come into the room than it pounced upon the badly carved mouse and paid no attention at all to the one that was carved so well.

There was nothing for the lord to do but give the gold to the unskilful carver, but as he did so he said: "Well, now that you have the gold, tell me how you did it."

"It was easy, my lord," said the man. "I didn't carve my mouse from wood. I carved it from dried fish. That's why the cat pounced upon it so swiftly."

When the lord heard how the cat and everyone else had been fooled, he could not help laughing, and soon everyone in the entire court was holding his sides with laughter.

"Well," said the lord finally, "then I'll have to give you two bags of gold. One to the workman who carved so well, and one to you who carved so cleverly. I'll keep the wooden mouse, and we'll let the cat have the other one."

The Dragon's Tears

Far away in a strange country there lived a dragon. And the dragon's home was in a deep mountain cave, from which his eyes shone like headlights. Very often, when some of the people living nearby were gathered in the evening by the fire, one would say: "What a dreadful dragon is living near us!" And another would agree, saying: "Someone should kill him!"

Whenever children were told about the dragon, they were frightened. But there was one little boy who was never frightened. All the neighbors said: "Isn't he a funny little boy!" When it was almost time for this funny little boy's birthday, his mother asked him: "Whom would you like to invite for your birthday party?" Then that little boy said: "Mother, I would like to ask the dragon!" His mother was very much surprised and asked: "Are you joking?" "No," said the little boy very seriously, "I mean what I say: I want to invite the dragon."

And, sure enough, on the day before his birthday the little boy stole quietly out of his house. He walked and he walked and he walked till he reached the mountain where the dragon lived.

"Hello! Hello! Mr. Dragon!" the little boy called down the valley in his loudest voice.

"What's the matter? Who's calling me?" rumbled the dragon, coming out of his cave. Then the little boy said: "Tomorrow is my birthday and there will be lots of good things to eat, so please come to my party. I came all the way to invite you."

At first the dragon couldn't believe his ears and kept roaring at the boy. But the boy wasn't frightened at all and kept saying: "Please, Mr. Dragon, please come to my party."

Finally the dragon understood that the boy meant what he said and was actually asking him, a dragon, to his birthday party. Then the dragon stopped roaring and began to weep. "What a happy thing to happen to me!" the dragon sobbed. "I never had a kind invitation from anyone before."

The dragon's tears flowed and flowed until at last they became a river. Then the dragon said: "Come, climb on my back and I'll give you a ride home!"

The boy climbed bravely onto the back of the ferocious dragon and away the dragon went, swimming down the river of his own tears. But as he went, by some magic his body changed its size and shape. And suddenly—what do you know!—the little boy was sailing bravely down the river toward home as captain of a dragon-steamboat!

—*by Hirosuke Hamada*

The Rolling Rice Cakes

Once upon a time there was an old man and his old wife. One day the old man said: "I'm going to cut some firewood today. Please make me some rice cakes for my lunch." So the old woman made rice cakes and put them in the old man's lunch box. Then the old man left the house.

He went far into the forest and cut firewood all morning. When it was noon, he sat down to eat and opened his lunch box, saying: "Now, for some of the old lady's delicious rice cakes."

Then he suddenly cried: "Oh, my!" because one of the rice cakes had fallen out of the box, and he saw it go rolling away. Away it rolled, and suddenly down it plopped into a hole in the ground.

The old man ran over to the hole and—what do you know!—he could hear tiny voices singing inside the hole. "What's going on down there?" he asked himself. "I'll drop one more rice cake down and see."

After he had dropped the second rice cake into the hole, he put his ear close to the ground, and now he could hear the words of the song. And this is the song the tiny voices were singing:

Rice cakes, rice cakes,
Nice, fat rice cakes,
Rolling, rolling, rolling—down!

"What a beautiful song," the old man said, and he kept rolling rice cakes down the hole until they were all gone. Then he leaned far over to peek into the hole.

Suddenly he called out: "Help! Help!" But it was too late—he had fallen in, and with a thump-thump-thump he too went rolling right down the hole.

There at the bottom of the hole he found hundreds of field mice. They had eaten all his rice cakes and now they were singing again as they pounded rice.

"Thank you very much for the delicious rice cakes, old man," the leader of the mice said. "To show our thanks we'll give you this bag of rice." And the mouse gave the old man a small bag of rice about the size of a fat coin purse.

"Goodbye, old rolling man," all the mice called. And then they sang another song:

> Nice man, rice man,
> Nice, fat mice man,
> Rolling, rolling, rolling—up!

And as they sang the old man felt himself rolling right up and out of the hole.

Once he was on top of the ground, the old man brushed himself off and then went home, carrying the small bag of rice with him.

When his old wife heard his story and saw the rice, she said: "Humpf! That won't make more than two or three rice cakes." But when she started pouring the rice out, they were surprised to discover that the bag always stayed full, no matter how much they poured out of it. It was a magic rice bag, a wonderful present that the mice had given them. After that they always had all the rice they could possibly eat. The old woman made rice cakes for herself and the old man every day—mountains of them—and they lived happily ever afterward.

The Robe of Feathers

Once there was a fisherman who lived all alone on a tiny island in Japan. He was very poor and very lonely. Early one morning he started toward his boat; there had been a bad storm the night before, but now the sun was shining brightly. As he walked along, he saw something hanging on a branch of one of the pine trees along the beach. It was beautiful and shining. He took it down from the branch and found that it was a wonderful robe made of feathers. The feathers were of all different colors, as lovely and soft as the rainbow, and they shined and sparkled in the sunlight like jewels. It was the most beautiful thing the fisherman had ever seen in all his life.

"Oh, what a beautiful robe!" he said. "It's certainly a priceless treasure. There's no one else on my island so it can't belong to anyone. I'll take it home and keep it always. Then my poor home will be beautiful and I can look at the robe whenever I'm lonely." Holding the robe very carefully in his rough hands, he turned and started to carry it home.

Just then a beautiful woman came running after him. "Mr. Fisherman, Mr. Fisherman," she called, "that's my robe of feathers that you're taking away. Please give it back to me." She went on to explain that she was an angel from heaven and that the robe of feathers was actually her wings. While she was flying through the sky, the storm had come and wet her wings so that she could not fly. So she had waited on this island until the sun came out and then had hung her wings out to dry on a pine tree, where the fisherman had found them.

"So you see," she finished, "if you don't give my wings back to me I'll never be able to fly back to my home in heaven again." Then the woman began to weep.

The fisherman felt very sad for her. "Please don't cry," he said. "Of course I'll give you your robe of feathers. If I'd known it belonged to anyone, I would never have touched it." And he knelt down before her and handed her the robe.

The angel began at last to smile and her face was shining with happiness. "Oh, thank you very much, Mr. Fisherman." she said. "You're

such a good man that I'm going to dance the angel's dance for you."

Then the angel put on the robe of many-colored feathers and began to dance there before the fisherman. It was certainly the most beautiful dance the fisherman had ever seen, and probably the most beautiful dance that had ever been danced anywhere on this earth, since angels usually dance their angel's dance high up in the heavens. The air was filled with heavenly music, and the feathered robe sparkled in the sunlight until the entire island was wrapped in rainbows.

As the angel danced, she rose slowly in the air, higher and higher, until finally she disappeared far up in the blue sky. The fisherman stood watching the sky and remembering the beautiful dance he'd seen. He knew that he'd never be lonely or poor again—not with such a beautiful memory to carry always in his heart.

The Princess and the Herdboy

This is a tale of long and long ago, when the King of the Sky was still busy making stars to hang in the heavens at night. The king had a very beautiful daughter. She was called Weaving Princess because she sat at her loom all day long every day. She wove the most delicate stuff in the world. It was so light and airy, so thin and smooth, that it was hung among the stars in the sky and draped toward the earth. It was the cloth that we now call clouds and fog and mist.

The King of the Sky was very proud of his daughter because she could weave so beautifully and was such a help to him. He was very busy making the sky, you see, and needed all the help he could get. But one day he noticed that Weaving Princess was becoming pale.

"Well, well, my little princess," the king said, "you've been working too hard I fear. So tomorrow you must take a holiday. Go out and play among the stars all day long. Then please hurry back and help me. I still need much more mist and fog, and many more clouds."

The princess was very happy to have a holiday. She'd always wanted to go and wade in the stream, called the Milky Way, that flowed through the sky. But she'd never had time before.

She put on her prettiest clothes and ran out among the stars, right over to the Milky Way. And there, in the middle of the stream, she saw a handsome boy, washing a cow in the water.

"Hello," the boy said to the princess, "who are you?"

"I'm the star Vega," she answered. "But everyone calls me Weaving Princess."

"I'm the star Altair," said the boy. "But everyone calls me Herdboy because I tend the cows that belong to the King of the Sky. I live over there on the other side of the Milky Way. Won't you come over to my house and play with me?"

So the herdboy put the princess on the back of the cow and led her across the stream to his house. They played all sorts of wonderful games and had so much fun that the princess forgot all about going home to help her father.

The King of the Sky became very worried when the princess failed to come home. He sent a magpie as his messenger to find her and tell her to come home. But when the magpie spoke to the princess she was

having such fun that she wouldn't even listen. Finally the king had to go himself and bring the princess home.

"You've been a very bad girl," the king said. "Just look at the sky—not even finished yet. You've been away playing and the sky needs clouds and mist and fog. So you can never have another holiday. You must stay here and weave all the time."

Then the king poured more and more star water into the Milky Way. Until now it had been a shallow stream that you could wade across, but the king poured in so much star water that it became a deep, deep river. The princess and the herdboy lived on opposite sides of the river, so now there was no way they could get across to each other.

So the princess went into her little house in the sky and sat in front of her loom. But she was so lonely and longed so much for her Herdboy that she couldn't weave at all. Instead she just sat there weeping all the time. And the sky became emptier and emptier, with no clouds, and no mist, and no fog.

Finally the king said, "Please, my little princess, you mustn't cry all the time. I really need clouds and fog and mist for my sky. I tell you what I'll do. If you'll weave again and work hard, I'll let you go and play with the herdboy one day each year."

The princess was so happy when she heard this that she went right to work, and she's been working very hard ever since.

But once each year, on the seventh night of the seventh month, the King of the Sky keeps his promise to Weaving Princess. He sends a flock of magpies to the Milky Way, and with their wings they make a bridge

across the deep river. Then the princess goes running across the bridge of magpies to where the herdboy is waiting for her. And they have wonderful fun playing together for one whole night and one whole day.

And that's the reason why Japanese children celebrate a holiday called Tanabata-sama, "The Seventh Night of the Seventh Month." Children everywhere love to play and it makes them happy to know that the Princess and Herdboy stars are having such fun together there up in the sky. So the children on earth decorate bamboo branches with bright pieces of paper and wave them in the sky, to remind the King of the Sky that it's time for him to keep his promise again.

Urashima Taro

A long, long time ago in Japan there was a young fisherman who lived by the seashore. His name was Urashima Taro. One day while he was walking along the beach, he saw that some boys had caught a big turtle from the sea and were teasing it and hitting it with sticks.

Now, Taro was very kindhearted and hated to see people being cruel to animals. So he said: "Boys, please let the turtle go. It's a nice animal and you shouldn't be mean to it. Put it back in the sea."

Then the boys were ashamed of themselves. They put the turtle back in the water and watched it swim happily away.

Several days later, Taro was again walking along the beach when he heard a voice saying: "Taro! Taro!"

He looked around, but couldn't see anyone. "Who is calling me?" he called out.

"Here I am," said a voice from the sea. It was a turtle, who came crawling up on the sand. "I'm the turtle you saved the other day. When I returned to the palace under the sea, I told the Sea Princess what you had done. This made her very happy, and she asked me to bring you to see her."

Taro said: "I've always wanted to visit the bottom of the sea." So he climbed on the turtle's back and was carried off very far and very fast to the great palace on the floor of the deepest sea.

He was taken inside the beautiful palace, which was made of coral and crystal, and there he met the beautiful Sea Princess. "Taro, you were very kind to my good subject, the turtle," she said to him. "I wanted to thank you, so I had him bring you here. Please be my friend and stay in the palace forever. We will be very happy, and you shall have everything you want."

So Taro stayed in the palace with the Sea Princess. He ate wonderful food, saw wonderful things and was very happy at first. But after awhile —after only a few days, he thought—he began to be lonely for his home and his friends back on the shore. He wondered how his father and mother were.

Finally, one day he said to the princess: "I've been very happy here, but I want to go back to the land and see my home and my friends. Please send me back."

"All right, Taro," the princess said, "if you are determined to go, then I'll send you back. But I'll be sorry to see you go. We've been so happy together. In memory of your stay here I'll give you this beautiful box. As long as you have this, you may come back to see me anytime you wish. But, Taro, don't open this, ever. If you open it, you'll never be able to come back. Be sure! Do not open it!"

So Taro took the box, thanked the princess for the wonderful time, climbed on the back of the turtle, and went back to his home.

When he got to the beach, the village had changed. He could no longer find his own house. He asked some people on the beach, "Where is Urashima Taro's house, and where are his parents?"

"Why, young man," they answered, "you're asking about things that were here many, many years ago. Urashima Taro was drowned before most of us remember. What strange person are you that you do not know this?"

Taro was very puzzled. How could this be? He was the same—or so he thought—and only the people and the place were different. Could it be that the secret of this strange thing was in the box that the Sea Princess had given him? He thought about this for some time, and then at last he decided to open the box, even though the Sea Princess had warned him not to do so.

He took off the lid, and a strange white smoke came out and curled about him. He touched his face and discovered that his face was all wrinkled and that he had a long white beard. Without realizing it, he had spent many, many years at the bottom of the sea, not just a few days. The magic box had kept him always young, but now the smoke from the box had turned him into the old, old man that he really was. All his friends were gone, and now that he had opened the box he could never return to the palace of the Sea Princess. He stood weeping on the shore.

The Fairy Crane

Once upon a time there was an old man who lived in the country all alone with his old wife. They had no children. One day the old man was walking along the road beside a rice field when he suddenly heard a strange sound: "Flutter, flutter, flap, flap." Following the sound, he discovered a beautiful white crane caught in a snare.

"Oh, you poor thing!" he said. "I will help you out." He set the crane free, and it flew away into the sky.

After the old man got home and was telling his wife about the crane, a knock came at the door and someone said in a sweet voice: "May I come in?" The old woman opened the door and there she found a pretty, dainty little girl.

The little girl said: "I have lost my way. Please let me stay in your house tonight."

The old people were very happy to have such a pretty girl in their house. And when she told them that she had no parents of her own, they asked her to become their daughter and live with them always. So the little girl stayed on with them.

One day the girl said to her new parents: "If you'll promise not to look at me even once while I work, I'll weave some cloth on the loom in the weaving room." Thereafter they could hear the sound of the loom every day—"Ton-ka-ra-ri, ton-ka-ra-ri"—and every night the little girl gave

them a beautiful piece of cloth which she had woven that day. It was the most beautiful cloth in the whole world and all the neighbors came to see it.

The old woman became more and more curious. She said to herself: "How in the world can this little girl weave such beautiful cloth?" So finally one day she peeked into the weaving room.

What a strange sight she saw! There, sitting at the loom, was not her little daughter but a beautiful white crane, using its own soft white feathers to weave cloth!

That night when the old man came home, the little girl came out of the weaving room and said: "I am the crane that you saved. I have been weaving cloth to repay the kindness you did for me that day long ago. But now that you have discovered my secret, I can no longer stay with you."

The old woman was sorry she had peeked, and the old man was in tears, but since they knew their daughter was actually a crane, they finally understood that she must go back to her home in the sky. "Goodbye, good luck," the girl said. And then suddenly she changed into a white fairy crane and soared gracefully up into the sky on her beautiful white wings.

The Old Man with a Wen

In a village in Japan there once lived a hard-working old man. On his right cheek he had a big lump called a wen. One day he went to the mountain to cut wood. Suddenly it began to rain.

"Good gracious! What shall I do?" he said to himself.

Then he was lucky to find a big hollow tree where he could wait till the rain stopped. While he was waiting, his head began to nod and he fell asleep. When he woke up, he was very surprised to find it was night already. In front of his tree a whole party of red and green elves were dancing.

"Aha!" cried one elf, "there's an old man in the tree." And they dragged him out of his hiding place.

"Now, old man, you must dance for us." So the old man danced his very best jig for the elves.

"Very good, very good! That was a lot of fun," said the elves, and they clapped their hands with glee.

"You must come again tomorrow night to show us your dance. Until then, we will keep your wen. Just to make sure that you do, we're going to take your wen and not give it back to you until you come and dance again." And they took the big lump right off the old man's face, thinking it must be something very precious.

The old man, of course, was overjoyed to lose his wen and left the forest singing.

When he got home, he told the story to his wife, who was both surprised and happy. Her old husband looked so handsome without his wen.

His neighbor next door also had an ugly wen and when he heard the story, he became very excited. "I could lose my wen in the very same way!" he said, and he went to the same mountain and hid in the same tree. At last, the same elves came for their party.

"Now is the time!" said the second old man, and he jumped out of the tree and began to dance.

But he could not jig as well as the first old man. The elves were not pleased and shouted: "This dance is not as good as the one we saw last night!" Finally one of them said: "Well, we don't ever want to see him dance again. Let's give him back his wen so he won't come again."

With that, the elves took out the wen they had taken from the first old man put it on his neighbor and chased him out of the forest. So the second old man went sadly home with two wens on his face instead of none.

The Flying Farmer

A long time ago there was an old farmer named Taro who lived in a village in Japan. Near Taro's house there was a wide, wet swamp where many wild ducks came to rest. Farmer Taro had made a trap out of rope, and he caught a duck almost every day.

Taro was very greedy and one night he thought to himself: "After all, only one duck a day isn't so much. How clever it would be to catch a whole lot of fine ducks at one time!"

So he made a great big trap out of a long piece of rope and fixed it so that he could catch many ducks at the same time.

Early in the morning of the next day Taro put out his new trap in the swamp. He held on to the end of the trap and hid behind a tree to wait for the ducks to come.

And then, all at once, a big flock of ducks flew down from the sky and landed right in the trap. "Tug! Twitch! Jerk! Pull! Tug! Twitch! Jerk! Pull!" Old Taro could see that he was catching many, many ducks, and he could feel them getting caught in the trap.

"Look! Look how many I have caught!" he cried, jumping up and down with glee.

About an hour later, when the sun was high in the sky, the ducks were ready to flyaway. Suddenly, "Whoosh!" and they all flew up into the sky at one time.

"Oh! Oh!" Old Taro was so surprised he hung on tight to the end of his rope trap and got carried right up into the sky with the ducks.

The whole flock of ducks flew together in one group way up high, and poor farmer Taro was terribly frightened hanging onto the rope and being carried along in the air.

On and on they flew, over mountains and everything. Finally they passed over a strange village where there was a tall green pagoda with five roofs.

The old farmer waited until he got a good chance; then he let go the rope and grabbed tight onto the spire of the pagoda as he flew by it. He held on tight to the spire and cried out: "Help! Help! Help me, someone!"

Soon a great crowd of people gathered around the bottom of the pagoda. They were certainly all surprised, and began talking all at once.

"How did he ever get up there?"

"Didn't you see the ducks carrying him?"

"What can we do to help him get down?"

After thinking it over, they brought a big, wide piece of cloth, and all held on to it and stretched it tight so that Taro could jump down into it. Then they all shouted up at him: "Jump down! Jump into this cloth! Jump!"

Taro looked down and was so frightened that his knees shook. But finally, he closed his eyes tight and jumped.

He was lucky and landed right in the middle of the cloth. But he was so heavy that all the round heads of the people holding the cloth were knocked together, "Bumpity, Bumpity, Bump!"

Just at that last "Bump!" Taro opened his eyes, and what do you think? He was home safe in his own bed. All this flying with ducks had been a bad dream.

But the dream seemed so real that it cured Farmer Taro of being so greedy. After that he never trapped any ducks at all and became a nice, kind gentleman.

Why the Red Elf Cried

No one knows now where the mountain was, but once there was a red elf who lived on a mountain that overlooked a village. This red elf wanted to make friends with the people who lived in the village, so in front of his house he hung a sign that read: "Everybody is welcome to come to my house and eat the good candy I will give them."

One day two woodcutters passed the red elf's house and saw the sign. One of them said: "Let's go in and get some candy." But the other said:

"No, no. That sign is only a trick so the elf can get us into his house and do something bad to us. Don't go inside!"

The red elf heard what the men said and called out through the window: "No, no. It's not a trick. Please come in and have some candy and be my friends." But the two woodcutters were frightened by his bright red face and ran away as fast as they could.

When the red elf saw that nobody would believe his sign he was very sad and started to take the sign down. Just then his good friend, the blue elf, came to visit him and asked why he looked so sad.

After the blue elf had heard the story, he thought for a while and then said: "I have a good plan for you. I'll go down into the village and make lots of trouble. Then you come and catch me while I am doing bad things and give me a beating. Then everyone will know you're a good elf and will want to be your friend."

So the next day the blue elf went down into the village and burst into a farmhouse. The farmer and his wife were so frightened they ran outside. Then the blue elf started breaking everything in the house. He had just broken the old woman's teapot and was just about to kick the farmer's dog when the red elf came running into the village. He grabbed the blue elf and pretended to give him a good beating. The blue elf cried with all his might.

The frightened people of the village stood at a distance and watched all this. Finally they said: "That red elf is a good elf after all. And he has lots of sweet candy at his house. So let's go and visit him often."

So the village people started going to the red elf's house. He was very happy to have so many new friends and he always gave them sweet candy and delicious tea. But then one day he suddenly remembered that in all this time his good friend, the blue elf, had not once been to see him. "Perhaps the blue elf is in some trouble," he said. "I'll go and see him."

Next day the red elf set out for the blue elf's house. It was far away in the mountains, but the red elf went there very quickly, riding on top of a little cloud. To his surprise, he found the blue elf's house empty and all shut up. He walked around the house several times, wondering what was the matter, and finally saw a note pinned on the front door. This is what the note said:

To my dear friend, the red elf:

I am so lonely that I am going away on a long journey. If we should keep on visiting each other the way we used to, the people in the village would know that we played a trick on them and that you didn't really beat me. So I will go far away and leave you with your new friends, the village people. Goodbye,

Your friend,
Blue Elf

The red elf read this note in silence two or three times. Then he burst into tears and cried and cried.

He had his new friends from the village and he knew he would be happy with them, but he also knew that he would always be sad when he remembered his lost friend, the blue elf, because it is good to make new friends, but it is also good to keep old friends. And this is why the red elf cried so hard.

— *by Hirosuke Hamada*

The Biggest in the World

Once upon a time, on an island in the ocean, there lived a big, big bird. He was big enough and strong enough to pick up a sheep, or even a cow, in one grab and fly up into the sky with it. This bird was very proud and was always boasting: "I'm the biggest in the world. If you looked all over the earth, you couldn't find another being as big and strong as I."

"Oh, no, Mr. Bird," said a sea gull one day who had just flown up from the south. "In a place in the Southern Sea there is a much larger being than you."

"What! What are you saying? Something larger than I am? You must be wrong! . . . All right, then, I'll just fly there right now, and we'll see who's biggest."

So the big bird flew off to the Southern Sea. But the Southern Sea is very wide, and no matter how far you go there seems to be no end to it. "Oh, but I'm tired!" the big bird said and started looking for a place to rest. Just in time, in the distance he saw two red columns sticking up out of the waves.

"This is just fine," the bird said, settling down with a sigh on one of the columns.

Just then the bird heard a terrible voice. "Hey!" cried the voice. "What's this? Who is sitting on the end of my feeler?" Then the column began to move, and suddenly, right from the middle of the waves, a huge lobster rose to the top of the sea, waving the feelers that the bird had thought were columns.

"Oh, what a terrible thing!" said the bird. Because he saw that the huge lobster was much, much larger than he. "I certainly lost this contest." And with that the bird flew quickly away home.

"Ho! ho! ho!" laughed the lobster. "I really frightened that bird. What fun to see the bird that thought he was so big run away like that. I'm truly the biggest in the world."

Just as the big lobster was saying this and feeling so proud, the sea gull happened to fly by. "Oh, no, Mr. Lobster," the gull said. "There is something still larger than you. You just swim farther south and you'll see."

"All right!" said the lobster, "that's just what I'll do. Such nonsense, saying there's anything bigger than I!"

So the lobster swam and swam. Finally, far to the south, right in the middle of the Southern Sea, he saw a huge mountain rising out of the water. And he could see two caves in the mountain.

"Ah ha!" he said. "Those are fine caves. They will make a good place for me, the biggest thing in the world, to sleep." And, happily wiggling his big feelers, he crawled up into one of the caves.

But what do you think! What Mr. Lobster had thought were caves in a mountain were actually the nose of a great whale!

"Oh, something's tickling my nose!" said the whale, because the lobster was wiggling his feelers inside the whale's nose. "Ka—ka—ka—choo!" the whale sneezed.

The poor lobster was blown high, high into the sky, and then he fell back down, right on top of a big rock sticking up in the ocean.

"Ouch! Ouch!" cried the big lobster. "My back is broken." Sure enough, his back was broken. And that is the reason why, ever since that time, all lobsters' backs are curved as though the shell were broken. And that's also the reason why you can listen and listen but never again will you hear a lobster say: "I'm the biggest in the world."

The Sandal Seller

Long ago there was an old man and his old wife living in the country. They were very honest, but very poor. One day, near the end of the year, they heard some children singing outside. This is the song the children sang:

Oh, Mr. New Year, are you coming near?

Why, yes, I'm just beyond the mountain here.

Oh, do you bring us gifts and things so nice?

Why, yes, I've "mochi" cakes of finest rice.

It made the old man and woman feel very sad and lonely to hear the children singing about New Year's. Because this year they had no money and couldn't celebrate the New Year.

"Oh, dear," the old woman sighed. "New Year's is the day after tomorrow. And we don't have any rice at all. So we won't be able to make any mochi cakes. We won't even have mochi to eat on New Year's Day, and New Year's is not New Year's without mochi."

The old man too sat sadly shaking his head. But then all of a sudden he got an idea. "I know what I'll take them to town right away and sell them. Then with the money we can buy some rice and make some mochi."

So the old man started out for town right away, carrying the straw sandals on a long pole over his shoulder. It was a very cold day, with a

strong wind and much snow. When he got to town he began to walk through the streets yelling: "Straw sandals! Straw sandals!"

But everybody was very busy and no one wanted to buy any straw sandals. He kept walking and walking, always yelling: "Straw sandals! Straw sandals!" But he never sold a single pair.

Just then another old man came along the street selling charcoal. He was yelling: "Charcoal! Charcoal!" The two old men met in the street and stopped to talk.

"How's your business?" asked the charcoal seller.

"Terrible!" said the sandal seller. "I haven't sold a single pair. Everybody's too busy getting ready for New Year's."

"I haven't been able to sell any charcoal either," said the other. "Come, let's walk together and see if we'll have better luck."

So they started walking together. "Straw sandals! Straw sandals!" one would yell. Then the other would yell: "Charcoal! Charcoal!"

But still they didn't sell any of the wares. It became later and later and their voices became weaker and weaker. It was also becoming much colder and snowing harder. Finally it was completely dark, and still they hadn't made a single sale, so they decided to stop and go home.

Then the charcoal seller said: "It's really too bad to take home the same things we started out with. Why don't we trade? Then you can take home my charcoal and I can take your straw sandals."

"That's a good idea," said the sandal seller. So they traded, and then each of them went to his home.

When the sandal seller reached home he was very, very cold. He told

the old lady the bad news—that he hadn't been able to earn a single penny. "But at least I have this charcoal," he said, "and we can get warm."

So they made a charcoal fire and then sat around it warming themselves. But they were so sleepy that they didn't notice a tiny elf that jumped out of the charcoal and hid in their closet watching them. The elf was scarcely an inch high, but he looked exactly like the charcoal seller the old man had met that day.

After the old man and woman had gone to bed, the elf came out of the closet and said: "I felt so sorry for this poor old man today that I gave him this magic charcoal. Every spark will turn into a piece of gold." Then the elf disappeared.

Sure enough, next morning when the old man and woman woke up, they found a great pile of gold beside the hearth. They were very surprised, but also very happy. They were able to buy plenty of rice and make very fine mochi for New Year's. And the old man never had to go out in the snow to sell straw sandals again.

The Singing Turtle

Once there were two brothers. One of them was very industrious. All day long he worked in the fields. He worked very hard, and he was never sullen nor unkind. He didn't particularly like to work, but his poor mother was ill and needed the little bit of money he could earn. So he worked without complaining, even when he was very tired. It was hard to get up in the morning and start working, but he did and always had a smile for his old sick mother. In the evening he was so tired he could

hardly walk home, yet he fixed her supper and tucked her in for the night before he allowed himself to sleep.

The other brother was quite different. He was very lazy. All day long, when he was supposed to be working, he lay on the grass or lazily picked flowers. And he was always sullen and often quite unkind. He didn't like to work and so he saw no reason why he should. When he needed money he'd go to his mother, and she would give him what little she could spare. But he was never satisfied and complained constantly. He slept all the time, yet he hated to get up in the morning, and he always shouted at his brother and snarled at his mother. In the evening he would come home for money and then go into town and stay half the night spending the money foolishly.

The family became poorer and poorer because, no matter how hard the industrious brother worked, the lazy brother spent their money all the faster. Finally, one spring morning, the first brother cut some firewood and said to his mother: "I'm going into town and see if I can't sell this wood to make some money, for we have nothing to eat for supper tonight." The sick mother said: "I hope you can, but don't work too hard or else you'll be sick like me." The lazy brother, who was lying on his back asleep in the sun, said nothing, but only snored loudly. So the industrious brother took the enormous load of firewood on his back and started for town.

He stayed all day but he couldn't sell a single stick of the wood. He was very discouraged and finally put the heavy wood on his back and started home, wondering how they would eat that day. The wood was heavy and his heart was heavier as he trudged through the forest. Finally he came to the little forest pond where he usually ate lunch and, putting the wood down by a tree, he sat down on a stump and began to cry.

He was a grown man and grown men don't cry very often, so he was very sad indeed. While he was crying he suddenly heard a voice. "Why

are you crying?" the voice asked. The young man looked all around but couldn't see anyone. "You'd better blow your nose," said the voice again. But he still couldn't see anyone.

"Where are you?" he asked finally.

"Right under the nose you'd better blow," said the voice. The young man looked down, and there was a turtle floating on a piece of wood.

"Did you speak?" asked the man.

"Naturally," said the turtle, "there's no one else around. Really, you'd better blow your nose."

"But turtles don't talk," said the brother.

"This one does. And what's more, I can sing too. I like singing."

"Sing?" he said.

"Blow your nose," said the turtle. After the young man had blown his nose, the turtle continued: "And I sing very beautifully too. But say, you're in trouble, aren't you?" The brother admitted that he was and finally told the turtle the whole story. After he had finished, the turtle said: "Well, you've fed me often enough, so I'll feed you now.".

"I've fed you?" asked the young man.

"Sure," said the turtle, "this is where you eat your lunches, isn't it? Well, I've been eating the crumbs you've dusted off your lap afterwards. And seeing as how you've fed me, now I'll feed you."

"You mean I'm supposed to eat you?" asked the man. "I don't think I could—not after our friendly talk and all, you know."

"No, no," said the turtle impatiently. "You take me into town, and I'll sing. Then the people will pay you much money."

The young man was undecided. "Can you really sing?" he asked.

The turtle only looked disgusted. "Of course I can—just listen," he said. And then he started to sing. Actually he couldn't sing very well, but a turtle that can sing at all is such an oddity that no one ever stops to think if he's singing well or not.

"That was wonderful," said the man and, picking the turtle up, started back to town with him.

The townspeople thought that the turtle was wonderful. They had never heard a turtle sing before, and after it had sung several songs they showered the turtle and the hard-working brother with coins. The young man took this money, bought food, and hurried back home with the turtle. When the mother saw the food she was very surprised. Her son told her what had happened, and the turtle nodded his head wisely from time to time. They were very happy, but just then the lazy brother showed up, and ate up all the food.

"You didn't make very much money," he complained. "If you'd give him to me I'd bring back a fortune."

"No, you wouldn't," said the industrious brother. "You'd run away with it. You can't have the turtle."

This made the lazy brother very mad and in no time at all they began to fight. The lazy brother knocked his brother down and took the turtle to town himself.

When the townspeople gathered, the wicked brother made them give him money. Then he held the turtle up in his hands and commanded "Sing!" But the turtle wouldn't sing a note. The brother became very angry and held him by his tail. "Sing!" he shouted. But not a sound came from the turtle. Finally the brother began whipping the turtle with a switch, but it didn't hurt the turtle at all. He just drew back into his tough shell.

At first the people laughed, but when they realized that the turtle wasn't going to sing, they became angry and wanted their money back. "This is just an ordinary turtle," they said.

"No, really, it's the same turtle you heard yesterday," said the wicked brother, becoming frightened. He hit the turtle's tough shell again and shouted: "Sing, sing!" Finally he began to plead: "Please sing, please!" But the turtle wouldn't sing a note.

The people became more angry and said: "Let's give this cheat a beating the same way he's beating that poor turtle." And they began to beat the wicked brother so hard that he howled with pain, because he didn't have a hard shell to protect him, you see. They beat him right out of town.

The turtle stuck out his head and crawled back to the house where the good brother and his mother lived. "Well, that bad man is gone," he said. "He got beaten and chased away. He'll never dare come back."

The mother and brother thought they ought to feel sorry, but actually they were relieved, and soon all three were laughing together.

Then the turtle looked shyly around the edge of its shell and said: "May I live with you? The other turtles think I'm a bit odd because I can talk, and sing. I'm more at home with humans. I can make money for you."

"Oh, please do stay," said the mother and the good brother. "Whether you can make money or not, we like you."

Thus it was that the turtle stayed and lived with them. He often sang in the town, and the three of them lived very happily on the money the townspeople gave to hear his singing.

Saburo the Eel Catcher

Once there was a man named Saburo who was a famous eel catcher. He was so expert that eels just couldn't resist his hook and so he always caught a lot of them. And when he caught one, he'd run right home and put it on the fire. Then when it was done, he would take it off the fire, put it on his rice, and eat it up, smacking his lips all the while. He thought that eels were delicious.

One day when he was fishing he felt a great pull on his line. "Oh, this one must be enormous!" said Saburo to himself as he pulled back with all his might. "Yo, heave, ho!" he shouted, and pulled out of the water just about the biggest eel that he had ever seen. "What an enormous eel!" cried Saburo, as the eel flashed out of the water. But he was pulling so hard that the eel flew right over his head and landed, with a big grunt, in the field behind him.

"Funny," said Saburo to himself as he looked for the eel. "Eels can't grunt. At least I don't think they can. Now, let's see. Where could he have gone to?" And Saburo began looking around the trees, in the tall grass, and under the big stones. But he couldn't find the eel anywhere. "Odd," he said, scratching his head. "I guess I pulled too hard and he went flying over the mountain." He kept on looking and suddenly saw

something big and long and black under a bush. "Aha," said Saburo rushing at it. But when he got there, he found it was only a big, black stick and no eel at all. "I never knew sticks and eels looked so much alike," he said, scratching his head.

Just then he saw a wild boar asleep in the grass. "Oh, my, I'd better be careful: wild boars are pretty dangerous." So he began tiptoeing around the sleeping boar, when all of a sudden he tripped over a stone and fell down with a thud. "Oh, that's done it!" said Saburo, trembling. The boar didn't move, though ordinarily the noise would have been enough to bring him charging through the grass at poor Saburo. So Saburo walked closer and saw the eel lying on top of the boar.

The boar was lying very still on its side, and the eel was sort of coiled on top with his head hanging over the boar's shoulder. "Oh, that's nice," said Saburo. "They've gone and made friends with each other. But I never knew eels and boars were friends before." But then he looked more closely and saw that the eel and the boar were both quite dead.

"Well, this is curious," said Saburo, "for I distinctly heard the eel grunt." Then he stopped, scratched his head and thought: "No, I know what it was. The eel landed on the boar and the boar grunted. That's more like it. Then the eel died because he was out of water and the boar died of fright." And that is just what had happened. The eel had gone sailing through the air, turning end over end, and had finally landed with a big thump right on the back of the sleeping boar. Now boars, even though they are fierce, are very sensitive. The surprise had been just too much for its nerves.

"Oh, what luck!" said Saburo to himself. "Both eels and boars are delicious. Oh, what a feast I'll have!" Then he stopped and wondered: "How on earth can I get the boar home tonight?" He scratched his head. "I guess I'll have to make something to carry that boar with. Here're some vines. I'll take some of these and use them to strap the boar onto my back and that way I can take him home."

So he pulled at the vines, but no sooner had he taken hold of one than it came loose and he saw it had wild yams on the end. "Oh, how wonderful," said Saburo, "wild yams. How delicious they will be!" Usually wild yams are hard to pull from the ground, but today they came loose as easy as anything.

Saburo said: "Now I have an eel and a boar and lots of wild yams, but I'll have to make something to carry the yams in. Here are some reeds. I'll use these." So he set to work picking reeds. He would grasp a thick top and pull violently; then they would come loose. He pulled one and it squawked once and then lay still in his fist.

"What's this?" wondered Saburo. "A reed with feathers?" But it wasn't, it was a pheasant—a nice, plump pheasant with a lovely green and red head, brown wings, and long, long tail feathers. "Well, what a nice bird you are," said Saburo patting its head, but the bird didn't move. In pulling he had wrung its neck. And there at his feet was a nest with thirteen big shiny eggs in it.

"Oh, thirteen must be my lucky number today," said Saburo. "Here I have a boar, an eel, lots of yams, a nice plump pheasant, and thirteen eggs! What a feast I'll have when I get home!"

Then he stopped. "But how to get them home I wonder," he said.

He thought and thought and thought about this big problem. There really seemed to be much more than one man could ever hope to carry. But he was determined not to leave any of these wonderful things behind him. Finally he took some of the reeds and wove a basket with them. He wove it wide and deep and strong, and then he

put the pheasant and the eggs in the basket, packing them carefully in moss. Then he put the boar across his back and tied it firmly with the vines. Then he tied the yams around his neck and let them hang down over his shoulders in the front. And finally, using still more of the strong vines, he tied the eel to one of his hands. When he was all finished, he was indeed a funny-looking sight, but everything was quite safe. And that's the way he went home, carrying the eel and the wild boar, and the yams, and the nice plump pheasant, and the thirteen eggs. All the way he kept imagining the wonderful feast he would have when he got home. His mouth was watering and he felt so happy that he didn't even notice how heavy a load he was carrying.

When he reached his house, he put all the things down on the kitchen floor and then just stood there thinking about what had happened to him. The more he thought about it, the funnier it seemed to him. He began to laugh a little, at first just a few chuckles, but soon he was rolling on the floor with laughter. When he could finally talk through his laughter, he said: "I'm a pretty good eel-catcher—that I am!" And laughed all the way through the wonderful feast he had that night.

What do you think? Don't you agree that Saburo was a pretty good eel catcher?

Kintaro's Adventures

Once there was a woodcutter and his wife living at the foot of a wild mountain called Ashigara. This woodcutter had once been a noble warrior and had lived in splendor in Kyoto, which was then the capital of Japan, but his enemies had become so strong that he finally had to flee with his wife into the mountains in order to save his life.

Soon after they came to live in the mountains the woodcutter's wife gave birth to a healthy, lively baby boy. The woodcutter was so happy that he named the baby Kintaro, which means "Golden Boy," saying that his

baby son was more precious than all the gold there was in Kyoto. His mother took one of her favorite jewels and hung it about the baby's neck. The jewel was made of a piece of red coral. Then she prayed: "Please help this baby boy to grow up to be a good man, a strong and healthy and fine man."

A few weeks after Kintaro was born, his father went far into the mountains one day to cut wood. His mother put the baby Kintaro in his crib to sleep while she went down to the mountain stream to wash some clothes. Suddenly, as she washed, she heard Kintaro crying loudly. "What can be the matter?" she said. And when she turned to look toward the cabin, she saw a terrible thing.

A huge bear suddenly came running out of the cabin, carrying the crying bear in his arms. Holding the baby tightly, but gently, the bear went running with it toward the mountains.

"Help! Help!" Kintaro's mother screamed with all her might. And she went running straight toward the bear.

When the bear saw the angry mother come running toward him, he

turned and jumped down a steep cliff, still holding Kintaro in his arms, and then went running down the valley toward the distant mountains.

"Help! Help!" the mother cried again. "Kintaro has been stolen."

Just then Kintaro's father returned. Seeing what was happening, he picked up his broad axe and went running after the bear. As he ran he kept shouting out for help and other woodcutters and farmers along the way joined in the chase, running after the bear with axes and sickles and clubs.

The bear ran faster and faster, and finally he reached a deep, deep ravine with a rushing river in it. The only way across the ravine was a long, narrow log. The bear ran nimbly across this log; then he stopped and picked the log up and threw it down in the river.

Then the people who were running after the bear couldn't get across. They stood screaming on one side of the ravine, and the bear walked calmly on to his home, carrying Kintaro with him.

The bear's house was a cave deep in the mountain. There in the cave the mother bear was crying because her baby cub had died right after he was born. Father Bear came into the cave and said: "Look! I've brought a baby back for you."

"Oh! What a darling!" Mother Bear said, taking Kintaro happily into her arms. She was so happy to have a baby to love again, and she took very, very good care of Kintaro, so that day by day he grew bigger and stronger.

Father Bear was the King of the Forest. All the animals of the forest came often to the cave with presents of berries, fruits, nuts, and honey.

Each time, Father Bear would bring Kintaro out to show him to the other animals. He would say very proudly: "Look! Isn't he a handsome healthy boy! Someday this boy will take my place as King of the Forest."

Thus Mother and Father Bear cherished their new son. Mother Bear fed Kintaro on bear's milk, and Father Bear taught him how to wrestle. By the time he was five, Kintaro could beat all the other animals at wrestling. He won easily from the monkey, and the fox, and the badger.

They all liked him so much that they helped and taught him everything that they could do.

After a few months of hard practice Kintaro learned from Uncle Deer how to make great leaps across the ground. And he could climb any steep cliff as easily as the mountain goat, leap wide rivers, run as fast as the rabbit, swim like the otter, and even see in the dark like an owl.

When Kintaro was about eight years old, Father Bear, the King of the

Forest, became very sick. Kintaro was very worried and went all over the forest to gather food and berries for Father Bear. But nothing did any good and Father Bear got sicker and sicker.

One day when Kintaro was at home in the cave taking care of Father Bear, a fierce, ugly wolf stuck his head in the entrance. He had come with many of his friends and servants. He glared in at the poor, sick bear and said: "Hey! You've become old and weak! You're no good any more. From now on I'm going to be king of this forest. Come, tell everyone that I'm their new king!"

The sick bear raised his head and looked at the wolf. "A mean thing like you can never become king," he said.

"All right, then," said the wolf. "I'll wrestle you, and if I win, then you'll have to admit that I'm the new king."

Father Bear got out of bed, ready to wrestle the wolf. But Kintaro

said: "You're too sick, Father Bear. Please let me wrestle the wolf in your place."

"No, no," said Father Bear. "I'm still King and I can still whip such an insolent wolf."

So the bear and the wolf started wrestling. The bear quickly caught the wolf in his strong arms and lifted him high over his head. "Now!" roared the bear, "how do you like this. If you don't give up, I'll throw you into the bottom of the ravine."

But just then the wolf's friends and servants all jumped into the fight too. They forced the bear to the ground and he couldn't get up, no matter how much strength he had.

"Oh, you cowards," cried Kintaro. And he jumped into the fight too. Letting fly with his fists, he beat up one wolf after another, until they all went running away into the forest, with their leader running the fastest of all.

"Thank you very much for saving me, Kintaro," said Father Bear. "You did very well. From today on, I make you King of the Forest. You must rule all the other animals justly and wisely and protect them from the wolves." And with these words Father Bear rolled over and died.

Thus Kintaro became King of the Forest.

And what had been happening back at Kintaro's real home all this time? His parents searched for Kintaro for a long time, but they could never find him and finally gave him up for lost. A little while later, a girl baby was born to them. They named the baby Misuzu, and one day, when she was just six years old, her mother called her to her side and gave her a jewel of white coral to hang around her neck.

"Listen to me very carefully," said her mother, "and I'll tell you something you must never forget. Before you were born, you had a brother named Kintaro, but he was stolen away by the bears."

"A brother!" said Misuzu. "Oh, how I should like to meet him."

"Perhaps you shall someday," said her mother. "If he is still alive, he should be wearing a coral jewel around his neck. It is just like yours, except red instead of white, and that way you'll be able to recognize him if you should ever see him."

One day a few days later, Misuzu went up on the mountain to pick some berries. But she couldn't find any good ones and kept walking and walking until at last she was far into the forest where she had never been before. All at once she saw a beautiful waterfall. And there in the pool at the bottom of the falls she saw a boy about eight years old playing with a bear and a monkey and some other animals. She looked and looked, and

suddenly she saw the boy was wearing a red coral jewel around his neck.

"Oh, it's my brother—it's Kintaro!" she cried. So she began shouting down to the boy: "Kintaro! Kintaro!"

Kintaro, now King of the Forest, was surprised to hear a human voice. It was a sound he couldn't remember ever having heard before. And he looked up toward the top of the cliff where Misuzu was. But he couldn't understand human speech and so could only look up at her, wondering what she was saying.

Then, all of a sudden, something made a rustling sound behind Misuzu. Just as she looked around, a wolf jumped out and grabbed her.

"Help! Help!" she cried, as the wolf started to carry her away.

"Oh, how terrible!" cried the monkey to Kintaro. "That's the little girl who lives at the foot of the mountains. We must save her from the wolf!"

So Kintaro and the monkey and all the other animals climbed quickly up the cliff and began running after the wolf.

The wolf, still carrying little Misuzu, ran across a log bridge over a deep ravine and was rushing away into the mountains.

"Stop! Stop!" they yelled after him.

The monkey reached the log bridge first and started to run across it. But just then the wolf grabbed a hornets' nest from a tree and threw it at the monkey. Hundreds of buzzing hornets flew at the poor monkey, and he was so surprised that he slipped right off the log and tumbled down into the rushing river, head over heels.

"Help! Help!" the monkey cried. He was a bad swimmer and was being swept away by the rushing torrent.

Kintaro didn't know what to do. Should he keep running after the wolf who was running away with the little girl, or should he stop and save

the monkey? Finally he said to himself: "I'll save the monkey first, because he's my good friend, and then I'll save the little girl."

He dived quickly into the stream and went swimming as fast as he could after the poor monkey. It was a terrible struggle, but Kintaro finally caught hold of the monkey and barely managed to pull him out onto a bank.

When they climbed out of the ravine, they couldn't see the wolf and the little girl anywhere. "What a shame!" said Kintaro. "In a minute we could have saved her." So he walked sadly back along the log bridge, and there he found a white coral necklace.

"The little girl must have dropped it," he said to the monkey. "Look, it's just like mine except that it's white instead of red."

"Oh," said the monkey, "that little girl must be your sister. She had a necklace just like yours, and she looked very much like you."

This made Kintaro want to save the girl all the more. So he called a big eagle, and told him: "Fly away and see if you can find the little girl."

The eagle flew up high into the sky and went whirling away. Presently he returned and told Kintaro: "The wolves have a castle over beyond the third mountain. They've locked the little girl in a tower at the top of the castle."

"All right then," said Kintaro, "let's go save her."

So Kintaro started for the wolves' castle. The bear and the wild boar

and the lion and the monkey and all the other animals of the forest went with him. The eagle flew in front of them, showing them the way.

Suddenly the great eagle came flying to Kintaro and said: "Quick! Quick! There's a forest fire and if we don't put it out right away, all the trees will be burned down."

Kintaro hurried over to the general of the wolves and said to him: "Quick! If we don't put out this forest fire, all the forest will be destroyed. You must come and help us."

"All right," said the wolf general. "Everybody follow me to the river, where we'll all wet our bodies."

So they all went to the river and jumped in. When their fur was completely wet, they climbed out of the river and ran and rolled on the grass in the path of the fire. By thus wetting the grass they hoped to keep the fire from spreading.

When the animals were wetting the grass some woodcutters came running up from the lowlands. The leader of the woodcutters was Kintaro's father. He and the other woodcutters cut down the trees in the path of the fire, and thus at last the forest fire was put out. Kintaro and his followers, and the wolves as well, breathed great sighs of relief. Just then Misuzu came running out of the wolves' castle.

"Father! How glad I am that you've come! That little boy there is my brother, Kintaro. Look! Isn't he wearing a red coral necklace just like my white one? He's become the King of the Forest. Let's hurry over and talk to him."

Misuzu led her father over to where Kintaro was. But Kintaro couldn't understand human speech. So by gestures Misuzu persuaded

Kintaro to come home with them. It was now ten years since Kintaro had been kidnapped from his home by the bear. But Misuzu gave him lessons every day, and soon he learned how to talk.

So, now, whenever Kintaro and his father go to work cutting trees in the forest, Misuzu comes and brings them tea while they rest. Just today she brought them their tea there and found all Kintaro's friends

waiting to drink tea and eat rice-dumplings with them. There was the monkey, and the deer, and the wolves, and many more.

When they saw her coming, they all cried out: "Oh, goody!" and then they began a feast, there in the beautiful forest where the autumn leaves were turning scarlet.

— Retold by Genichi Kume